More Than a Hat

By Maggie Bridger
Illustrated by Jamie Smith

More Than a Hat
Copyright ©2001 The McGraw-Hill Companies, Inc.
By Maggie Bridger
Illustrated by Jamie Smith

SUNSHINE™ is a trademark of The McGraw-Hill Companies Inc.

Wright Group/McGraw-Hill
19201 120th Avenue NE
Bothell, WA 98011
www.WrightGroup.com

Printed in China through Colorcraft Ltd, Hong Kong

10 9 8 7 6 5 4 3 2 1

ISBN: 0-322-04512-6
ISBN: 0-322-04608-4 (6-pack)

CONTENTS

CHAPTER 1
More Than a Hat

Nic wanted to be a detective,
just like his sister Lina.
He had a notebook and pen,
just like Lina. He had a desk
and a magnifying glass,
just like Lina.

"May I be a detective
with you?" he asked Lina.

"No," said Lina.

Nic looked at Lina.
What made her a detective?
What did she have
that he didn't have?
A hat!
A special detective's hat!
Maybe if he had Lina's hat,
he could be Lina's partner.

When she wasn't looking,
he tiptoed up,
snatched her detective's hat,
and ran away with it.

"Nic!" Lina yelled.
"Give me back my hat."

Nic raced around the house.
He ran into the kitchen.
He hid behind the brooms and
the mops.
"Lina will never find me here,"
he told himself.

But Lina found him.

"It takes more than a hat
   to be a detective," she said.
"You have to look for clues.
   You have to keep trying.
   You have to remember
   everything you see and hear."

"I can learn how to do that,"
   Nic said. "Will you show me?
   Please?"

"Okay," Lina said.
"It might take years,
   but I will try.
   We'll start tomorrow."

Bring something for digging

CHAPTER 2
The Dig

The next morning,
Lina handed Nic a map.

Nic looked at the map.
"This is easy to read," he said.
"I'm supposed to dig in the sand.
It's easy to be a detective."

"Maybe," Lina said.

Nic ran to the park.
When he saw the sand pile,
he gulped.
"I forgot how much sand
there is!" he said.
Nic dug in one place.
Then he dug in another spot.
"I will keep trying,
but this could take years!"
he said.

Then he remembered to look
for clues.
Some of the sand was not
as smooth as the rest.
As soon as he started to dig
at that spot, Lina took off
her hat and sweater and began
to write in her notebook.

Other kids watched Nic digging.
"What are you doing?"
Hiro asked.
Hiro lived down the street.
He was a detective, too,
but he never helped Lina.

"I'm being a detective," Nic said.

"We don't need another detective
in this neighborhood," Hiro said,
and he walked off.
The other kids stayed.
Zeke, a big dog, scratched
at the sand.
He wasn't helping much,
so Nic was glad
when Zeke went away.

Finally, Nic's fingers felt
something different than sand.

It was a box.
Nic dug it out.
When he opened it,
he found…

...a hat, just like Lina's.

"Now we can be detectives together," he said.

"Not yet," Lina said.
"You still have a lot to learn.
It will take years and years."
She picked up her sweater and shook the sand off it.
"But someday..."

Lina stopped.
"What's wrong?" Nic asked.

"My hat!" Lina said.
"It's gone!"

CHAPTER 3
Keep Trying

Nic put his new hat
on his head.
"This one is mine," he said.
"It still has a tag."

Lina looked at the tag.
"Yes," she said.
"That one is yours.
Let me think.
Where could my hat be?"

Nic thought.

"There were lots of kids around," he said.

"Yes," Lina said.
"Hiro was here.
He says he is a detective,
but he doesn't have a hat
like mine.
Let's go talk to him."

They walked over
to Hiro's house.
Hiro was sitting
on the front porch.

"He didn't take your hat,"
  Nic said to Lina.
"He has his own hat."

"Why would I want your hat?"
  Hiro asked.
"I like to be able to see
  where I'm going."

Nic and Lina went back
to the park.
"Who else might have my hat?"
Lina asked.

Nic thought back.
"Zeke dug for a while," he said.
"Maybe he took your hat."
They went to see Zeke.
The dog was chewing—
but not on a hat.

"Uh-oh," Nic said.
"I'll have to find another
spoon for the kitchen."

CHAPTER 4
Remembering

Nic and Lina walked back
to the park.

"Where can my hat be?"
Lina asked.

"Wait a minute," Nic said.
"Tell me again. What does it take
to be a detective?"

"You need to look for clues
    and think hard," said Lina.
    Nic nodded. He was thinking
    very, very hard.

"You need to keep trying,"
    said Lina.
    Nic nodded again.
    They had talked to Hiro.
    They had found Zeke.
    They were trying again and
    again.

"And you need to remember
    everything," Lina said.
"Now I'm going to talk
    to all the other kids.
    Maybe they saw my hat."

Nic didn't nod.

He was remembering.

Lina had her hat on when they got to the park.

Nic started digging, and then Lina started taking notes.

Did she have her hat on then?

No!

Where had she put her hat?

Nic looked at all the sand
that had come out of the hole.
Then he started digging.

"I've found it!
I've found your hat!"
he yelled.

Lina ran back.
"Where was it?" she asked.

"Under the sand!" Nic said.
"I remembered! When I was digging,
you put your hat down,
and I covered it up."

Lina shook the sand
out of her hat
and put it on her head.

"Well, partner," she said.
"It takes more than a hat to
  make you a detective.
  It takes using your head!"